For Charlie, who is never naughty ever

Magic and Mischief

STACY GREGG

HarperCollins *Children's Books*

First published in Great Britain by
HarperCollins *Children's Books* in 2021
HarperCollins *Children's Books* is a division of HarperCollins*Publishers* Ltd
HarperCollins Publishers
1 London Bridge Street
London SE1 9GF

www.harpercollins.co.uk

HarperCollins*Publishers*
1st Floor, Watermarque Building, Ringsend Road
Dublin 4, Ireland

1

ISBN 978–0–00–840281–5

Stacy Gregg and Crush Creative assert the moral right to be identified as the
author and illustrator of the work respectively.

A CIP catalogue record for this title is available from the British Library.

Typeset in Cambria Regular 12/24
Printed and bound in England by CPI Group (UK) Ltd, Croydon CR0 4YY

MIX
Paper from
responsible sources
FSC™ C007454

Chapter One

It was like Christmas. No, better than that – it was like every single Christmas *ever* all at once! Olivia had hardly been able to sleep last night, after her mother had said they could have riding lessons. Now, as the car turned down the lane and the stables lay up ahead, she gave a strangled squeak.

'Ha ha!' Ella piped up from the back seat. 'Livvy sounds like a meerkat!'

'Ella, don't be horrid to your little sister,' said Mrs Campbell.

Ella snorted. 'You've already moved us to the middle of nowhere *and* taken away my mobile phone. How much more can you punish me?'

'You'll grow horns if you use your phone too much,' Mrs Campbell replied. 'I read it in the paper. Children are sprouting them on the back of their heads from spending all day on their devices. And that, Ella, is exactly why we moved here. There's no need to be glued to your screen when you have all this countryside to play in and such lovely fresh air!'

Mrs Campbell said the word *devices* as if they were poison and *fresh air* as if she was about to burst into song.

'I don't know why I had to come today.' Ella continued her grumbling from the back seat. 'I don't even like horses!' But up front Olivia wasn't paying her big sister the slightest bit of attention. She was utterly transfixed by the stone buildings covered in ivy up ahead and the sign above them that read:

PEMBERLEY STABLES

'Do you think we should have phoned ahead back when we were in Pemberley village? What if all the horses are busy?' she asked.

'I tried the stables' number, but there was no answer,' her mum replied. 'If they're too booked up to give you a lesson right now, we can always make arrangements to come back.'

It seemed miraculous to Olivia that the stables were just down the lane from their new house. After the divorce, when Mrs Campbell had announced to her daughters that they were leaving London and moving to the country, Olivia's first thought had been, *PONIES!* And now here she was, about to have her first-ever riding lesson. It was a dream come true!

'This is my worst nightmare,' Ella groaned as Mrs Campbell pulled up in front of the stable block. 'I'm staying in the car.'

'Don't you want to meet the ponies?' Mrs Campbell asked.

'No,' Ella sighed. 'I want to play games on my phone. Can I have it back, please?'

'Do you *want* to grow horns, Ella?' Mrs Campbell tutted. 'Come on. You can have a lesson too if you

want. Otherwise you'll be bored sitting here doing nothing.'

Ella got out reluctantly and dragged her feet as she walked, scuffing them on the pebbles on the driveway as Olivia bounded ahead like an excited Labrador.

The doors at the entrance of the stable block were shut.

'Hello?' Mrs Campbell called out. 'Anyone here?' She gave a hearty rap on the doors, but there was no reply.

'It's closed,' Ella said with obvious satisfaction. 'Oh well, never mind!'

'But, Mum!' Olivia begged. 'Please!'

Mrs Campbell tried pulling on the heavy wooden doors, but they refused to budge even slightly. 'I'm sorry, Livvy,' Mrs Campbell said with a sigh, 'but the place is locked up.' And she turned and followed Ella, who was already marching back to the car.

Olivia, on the verge of tears, was about to go after them when she heard the whinny of a pony. The whinny sounded so very sad that Olivia couldn't just ignore it and walk away. She went back to the stable doors and tried them once more and, to her surprise, they flew open in her hands. Olivia looked around. Her mum and Ella had already reached the car and so she slipped inside.

In the darkness Olivia blinked as her eyes became accustomed to the gloom.

'Wow!' she gasped as she took in the sight before her. Even covered with dust and cobwebs, the place looked amazing. The stables must once have been very elegant with cobbled floors and looseboxes on either side of the central corridor. Olivia walked down the row and looked inside each box. Where had the whinny come from? She had hoped there might be a pony in here somewhere, but the stables were clearly long abandoned. Each stall had mounds of dusty straw on the floor. From the rafters above her came the fluttering sound of bats.

'I bet it would have been super amazing back in the olden days,' Olivia whispered. 'Imagine! Beautiful horses in every stall . . .'

'Oh yes, it was glorious! Truly glorious!' a voice behind her agreed.

Olivia spun round. There was a girl standing there. She looked about nine years old, the same age as Olivia. Later, Olivia would think that her clothes were very curious, all things considered.

Olivia had tried to dress the part that day, wearing stretchy jeans and boots, and tying her thick brown hair back in what she hoped was a smart ponytail with a tweedy headband.

This girl, on the other hand, looked like she was almost ready for bed. She was wearing a white nightgown that was very old-fashioned and flouncy, with enormous puffy sleeves and lace. She had green eyes, flaming red hair in a tumble of spiral curls that she had tied back in a messy bun, and freckles on her pale cheeks. She seemed surprised that Olivia had turned round and even more shocked that Olivia was now speaking to her.

'Hello!' Olivia said. 'I thought this place was empty. Sorry for just letting myself in! Do you work here?'

'You can see me?' the girl said.

Olivia thought this was an odd thing to say. 'Well, yes. Of course!'

'And you opened the doors? All by yourself?' The girl frowned.

'Um, yes, I did.'

The girl's eyes widened. 'Nobody has ever been able to come inside before,' she said, staring very hard at Olivia. 'What's your name?'

'I'm Olivia.'

'Well, Olivia,' the girl said, 'I'll wager that you must be especially brave.'

It was another strange thing to

say, but even stranger was the fact that the girl was right. It was well known that Olivia was quite fearless. From the day she was born Mrs Campbell had been driven to despair by Olivia's heroic nature. She only had to turn her back for a second and Olivia would be climbing a tree to rescue a kitten or clambering down a drainpipe to help an injured water vole. She was a whizz on roller-skates and a demon on her bicycle, but, despite all kinds of risky adventures, she had never once broken a bone or ever so much as a fingernail. So, yes, Olivia was brave. But she had no idea what this had to do with opening doors!

'I suppose I might be,' she admitted.

'*Ooooh!*' The red-haired girl clapped with glee. 'I knew it!'

Then, with great seriousness, she looked at Olivia and said, 'Go now. Your mother is waiting and

I expect she's getting cross about it. If I've learned anything in the past two hundred years, it's that you should never make your mama angry. So leave now, but please promise me that you'll come back?'

Two hundred years? What does she mean by that? Olivia thought to herself, but at that moment there was the honk of a car horn outside. Olivia turned, startled by the noise, and, when she turned back again, to her surprise the girl with the red hair had gone.

'I'll come back,' she whispered into the darkness. 'Pinkie promise.'

Chapter Two

Olivia spent the rest of the afternoon thinking about the girl with the red hair and the promise she had made. That night she went to bed early, telling her mum that the fresh country air had exhausted her, but in her room she prepared her escape. She stuffed what she hoped was a convincingly Olivia-shaped pillow under her duvet to make it look like she was tucked in and fast asleep. Then she pulled on a thick woollen jumper, grabbed the torch from her bedside table and promptly climbed out of the window.

Her heart was racing as she ran in the dark down the lane to Pemberley Stables. Her shoes crunched on the gravel of the driveway until at last she reached the heavy wooden doors. Once again, when she pushed them, they opened for her, just as they'd done before.

Olivia stepped inside. The light from her torch illuminated the darkened stables. She followed the beam and gave a gasp when she saw a pair of glowing eyes staring straight back at her!

Whooooooo!

There was a ghostly sound, then the flapping of wings as the barn owl that she had just startled flew up to hide in the rafters.

'Oh crumbs!' Olivia clasped her hand to her chest. 'You gave me a fright! I thought you were—'

'Hello there!'

Olivia shrieked and almost dropped her torch! Glowing in the light of the beam was the red-haired girl.

'You came back!' the girl said with a smile. 'I'm so glad. I was really worried that I'd scared you away.'

'You're here very late! Do you live here?' Olivia asked.

'Of course!' the girl said brightly. 'I should have introduced myself before. I'm Eliza. I look after the ponies.'

'Ponies?' Olivia was confused. 'But I looked through the entire stables. All the stalls were empty . . .'

As Olivia said this, a distant, ghostly whinny echoed through the night air. 'Was that a pony?'

Olivia shivered. 'It sounded very strange!'

'Well, it *is* all a bit strange,' said Eliza, frowning. 'There's something about the ponies that I need to explain,' she said, 'but perhaps it's easiest if I show you.'

She beckoned Olivia to follow her and the two girls went back out through the stable doors. By the entrance the ivy grew dense and tangled over the ancient stone.

'Help me push the ivy back, Olivia,' Eliza said. 'I'd do it myself, but look . . .'

Eliza waved her hand at the wall, trying to grasp the ivy, but her fingers disappeared straight through them as if they were made of fog!

'I can't touch anything. It's dreadful!' she groaned. 'It can be so frustrating.'

'I can imagine!' Olivia said.

She grasped the leaves and wrenched the vines

23

apart to see that there were words carved into the stone of the wall.

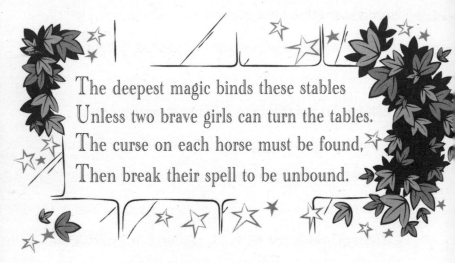

The deepest magic binds these stables
Unless two brave girls can turn the tables.
The curse on each horse must be found,
Then break their spell to be unbound.

'It's a very strange poem,' Olivia said with a frown.

'Well, not a poem exactly,' Eliza said. 'It's more like, um, a spell.'

Olivia was shocked. 'A spell!'

'I'm afraid so.' Eliza sighed. 'It's a witch's spell and a rather good one. My mother, Lady Luella, paid the Pemberley Witch six gold coins to cast it, which was quite a lot of money in those days. For such a grand sum the witch promised her a spell that would be almost impossible to break. And it is. Goodness only knows I've tried myself *so* many times for *so* very long now!'

'I don't understand.' Olivia was puzzled. 'Why would your mother pay a witch to do such an awful thing?'

'She did it for the most powerful reason of all,' Eliza said. 'Because of a broken heart.' And at that moment Eliza herself looked for all the world as if her own heart was about to break. She turned her face away from Olivia as she spoke once more. 'Can you keep a secret, Olivia?'

'Yes.'

Eliza reached out towards the other girl to hold her hand. Then stopped. 'Do you promise?'

Olivia gulped. 'I do.'

Eliza nodded. When she spoke again her voice was suddenly so ghostly that the echo of her words seemed to make the night grow darker around them.

'Good. Our secret is held fast and sealed and now at last I can reveal . . . the curse of Pemberley Stables.'

Chapter Three

Olivia had heard ghost stories before, but she had never had one told to her by an actual ghost!

'Two hundred years ago,' Eliza began, 'when my mother, Lady Luella, was the mistress of Pemberley Manor, these stables were very grand. Mama was an excellent rider and we kept the most amazing horses. It was all so glorious . . . until one fateful day.' Eliza bit her lip. 'It was a fox hunt. The first of the season. There was frost zinging in the air as Horace, the Hunt Master, gathered the hounds on the lawn of the manor. All the lords and ladies were there, drinking hot stirrup cups and laughing gaily. I had begged Mama to let me come too. I was a very good rider so she had agreed – as long as I stayed to the rear of the field.

'But, on the hunt, it all got too exciting for my pony, Chessie, to hang back and so we rode on, up ahead of Horace the Hunt Master, which is very bad etiquette, but never mind. Anyway, it was all going swimmingly until . . . right in front of a massive hedge, just as Chessie was about to jump . . .'

Eliza's eyes filled with tears. 'There was a rabbit hole. Completely hidden from sight. Chessie stuck his leg straight into it and fell. It was the most horrible, terrible accident! Not Chessie's fault at all! There was no one to blame for what happened that day. Except maybe, I suppose, the rabbit who dug the hole, now that I come to think of it. But then that's what rabbits do, don't they? So not even the rabbit can be blamed. Not really. It was just awful, rotten, bad, bad luck. But my mother blamed my pony, you see? She was so very distressed and utterly inconsolable. After I died, she vowed never to ride again. And she despised the ponies! That was when she visited the Pemberley Witch and asked her to come up with a spell to bind them.'

'So the ponies are ghosts?' Olivia asked.

'Not ghosts – they're as real as when the curse was cast. They're just spellbound,' said Eliza. 'Ponies who are stuck in time. The witch's magic has trapped them until, one by one, each pony can prove their worth. The spell made them all naughty in their own way, so we need them to become good again.' Eliza looked forlorn.

'Does the spell hold you too?' Olivia said.

'I suppose so.' Eliza looked as if she'd never considered this before. 'I've been here ever so long now. But today, for the first time in all those years, I feel as though I've found a way at last to break the curse of Spellbound Stables so the ponies can come alive again, if you'll help me.'

'Me?' Olivia was puzzled.

'Well, you and me,' said Eliza. 'The two brave girls in the poem!'

Olivia's heart was pounding as she considered what Eliza was saying. 'So, if we fix the ponies' problems, the stables will be restored to how it was before?'

'Exactly!' Eliza said. 'Each pony is under a different enchantment. We'll need to call them forth one by one, break the spell and – *hey presto!* – the curse of Spellbound Stables will be lifted at last!'

'Imagine it!' Olivia said. 'We'd have a whole stable full of real-live ponies!' It was all she'd ever wished for. 'Let's do it!'

'Oh, hooray!' Eliza threw herself at Olivia to give her a hug and Olivia felt a strange, misty whoosh as Eliza's arms swept straight through her. Then Eliza was on the other side!

'Oops!' she giggled. 'Come on then! Let's start straight away!'

The two girls went back inside the stables and stood before the first stall.

'What now?' Olivia asked.

'To summon a pony you simply walk across the threshold of its stall and read out the name on the door at the same time,' Eliza said. 'Come on. Try it!'

Olivia peered at the door. In the darkness the brass plaque began to glow with an unearthly light and words began to appear.

'It's working!' Olivia said.

She felt a chill run through her as the name materialised before her eyes. Then, with her heart racing, she stepped over the threshold and spoke the words out loud.

'Bad Bess.'

Chapter Four

*A*n icy mist rose from beneath Olivia's feet, making her shiver as it swirled up her legs until it filled the whole stall and she couldn't see a thing!

Then, just as quickly as it had come, the fog disappeared. And there, right in front of Olivia, where a moment ago the stall had been empty, stood a horse.

Bad Bess was the colour of a starless sky at

midnight. Her coat was lustrous, her mane long and glossy, and her tail was so thick and long it swept out behind her like a black bridal veil.

'Oh wow,' Olivia breathed. 'She's beautiful!'

The mare gave her tail a theatrical swish. *'Why, thank you!'* she said. *'I do so love compliments!'*

Olivia was stunned. 'You can speak?'

'I know!' said Bess. *'It's the coolest, right?'* She gave her tail another vigorous twirl. *'I'm Bess,'* she said. *'What's your name?'*

'Olivia, but my friends sometimes call me Livvy.'

'Are we friends?' the mare asked.

'I hope so,' Olivia said. 'I've come to help you.'

'Oh good!' And then the horse looked confused. *'Help me with what exactly?'*

Eliza, who had been standing with Olivia as all this was going on, gave a heavy sigh. 'With the spell, Bess,' she said, as if she was explaining it for the umpteenth time, which Olivia suspected she was. 'Remember we've talked about this? About how you have a spell on you?'

'*Oh yes!*' Bess said brightly, as if spells were a good thing. '*So . . . what do we do to get rid of it?*'

'I'm not sure exactly,' Olivia admitted. 'You're the first horse that I've tried to break the spell for. Perhaps we could begin with your problem. What is it that's wrong with you?'

'*Hmm.*' Bess thought about this. '*There's nothing wrong with me.*'

'Bess!' Eliza groaned. 'Yes there is! Tell Olivia what you do!'

'*Oh right!*' Bess giggled. '*Well, I'm a highway horse, you see.*'

'A highway horse?' It was Olivia's turn to be confused now. 'What's that?'

'*Well –*' Bess lowered her voice to a whisper as

if she was telling Olivia a secret – *'every night, when the clock strikes midnight, I get dressed in my outfit . . . '* Bess flicked her tail towards the black mask and cape that were hanging on the wall.

'And then,' she continued, *'I go out and wait for the coachman to come. When I hear his horses and I see his outline in the moonlight, I gallop like mad! And, quick as a flash, just like that, I cut the carriage off and make them stop. I yell out, "Stand and deliver!" Ooooh, it's very dramatic! Quite exciting, in fact. So I say those words and then I look deadly serious and everyone inside the carriage gives me lots of things. And I stuff all their possessions into my sack. And, once the sack is full up, I take it all to Horace.'*

'Who's Horace?' Olivia asked.

'Horace is the Hunt Master,' Eliza spoke up. 'Remember how the spell began with that dreadful accident with the rabbit hole on the hunting field? Well, when I cut in front of him Horace and his horse fell that day too, and he broke his neck. It's very peculiar actually. His head is still hanging in there, but it's quite wobbly.'

'*It jiggles about when he gets cross,*' Bess agreed.

Eliza sighed. 'Anyway, it all happened positively ages ago, but Horace is still surprisingly furious about it! He's such a grumpy ghost! And he's always up to no good, encouraging the ponies to keep to their troublesome ways and spooking anyone who dares to come round here. If he had his way, all the horses in the stables would remain spellbound forever.'

'Taking things, *stealing* things, is naughty, Bess,' said Olivia.

'*But I don't think so, and Horace doesn't either!*' Bess chortled. '*He loves it when I steal!*'

'I bet he does,' Olivia muttered under her breath. 'So this Horace – tell me, do you work for him?'

'In a way, I suppose,' Bess said. *'He doesn't pay me or anything. I take him the sack each night – full of wonderful things like diamond necklaces, pearl earrings and gold coins. The booty! That's what Horace calls it. And then I come home again and I have my feed and, when my tummy is full, I cuddle up with Raymond. And then I go to sleep.'*

'Raymond?' Olivia felt like she was doing nothing but asking endless questions. 'Who's Raymond?'

From beneath the fog Bess reached down, and when she raised her head she had a teddy bear in her teeth.

'This is Raymond!' she said, proudly holding up a scruffy stuffed bear so that Olivia could see him. *'Isn't he totally gorgey? Raymond is my very best*

friend. I couldn't possibly sleep at night without

him, could I, my little snugglekins?'

Bess gave her teddy a smooch and popped him

back down in the fog again.

'Right!' Olivia said. 'Well, thanks for that, Bess.

I've heard enough for now. I think I know what your

problem is.'

'*You do?*' Bess brightened up even more. '*Oooh goody! What is it?*'

'You're a thief,' Olivia said.

'*Well, yes,*' Bess agreed.

'So you have to stop it.'

'*No,*' Bess replied.

'No? What do you mean, no?' Eliza frowned.

'*I like taking things. It's fun. Besides, that's what I do,*' Bess said. '*I'm a highway horse, you see?*'

'Yes, but stealing is naughty,' Olivia said.

'*Is it, though?*' Bess mused.

'This is impossible,' Olivia murmured to Eliza. 'How are we going to help her if she doesn't even want to change?'

'*Quite true! Very tricky,*' agreed Bess who, with a sparkling flash of her tail, had magically dressed herself so that the black mask covered her face and the velvet cape was draped round her neck.

'*It's quite the bind you're in*,' Bess continued to burble. '*Very hard to help me if I don't want to be helped. Must be dreadful for you. Anyway, the thing is, it's almost midnight now so I must dash. I've got some highway robbery to do . . .*'

As Bess bustled past, Olivia felt the pony nudge against her. She turned to Eliza in astonishment. 'She's real!'

'Oh yes,' Eliza confirmed. 'Once you summon them, they're quite real indeed. But they can disappear again at will if you make them cross. That's why the spell makes them so very tricky to handle.'

'We need to stop her!' Olivia said.

'I know!' Eliza agreed.

'No!' Olivia cried. 'I mean, we need to stop her right now! Look – she's getting away!'

But it was too late! The chime of hooves rang

through the stable corridor as Bess bolted for the front doors.

'*Ta-ta for now!*' Bess called back to them. '*It's time for crime!*' And then she was off and galloping up the lane with her cape flying in the night air behind her as she disappeared into the blackness beyond.

Chapter Five

Changing schools and making new friends was always going to be a challenge. That was what Mrs Campbell had said to Olivia when they'd moved house. So how come Ella already seemed to have loads of friends and Olivia had no one?

At lunchtime, awkward and alone, Olivia found a spot hidden far away from the others behind an old oak tree, and sat down on the grass.

'Hi!' Eliza walked straight through the tree, then flopped down beside her.

'*Eeek!*' Olivia leaped up as if she'd sat on a wasp and Eliza shrieked and jumped up as well.

'What is it?' She looked around wildly as if she was expecting danger from all quarters. 'What's there?'

'You are!' Olivia groaned. 'You popped up out of nowhere!'

'Oh!' Eliza giggled. 'Sorry about that! You looked like you'd seen a ghost! Anyway, I've come to see you,' she continued, 'because I think we should have another go at convincing Bess. Surely if we explain to her why stealing is wrong, and downright naughty, she'll understand? Would you come back again tonight and try?'

'Sure,' Olivia agreed. 'If you think it will help. She looked at Eliza all pale and shimmery in her white nightie.

'I could bring you some of my clothes to change into if you'd like? Instead of that ghostly gown.'

'Ooh, would you?' Eliza said brightly. 'I'd adore that! So I'll see you later then?'

'Do you have to go right away?' Olivia said. 'Can't you stay and play?'

'I suppose I could sit awhile,' Eliza said. 'Shall we make daisy chains? I used to love doing that.'

Olivia made herself a chain so long she could wear it as a crown. She made one for Eliza too, but when she tried to put it on her the daisies kept falling through Eliza's head.

'Someone's coming,' Eliza pointed out.

Olivia looked up to see Ella striding towards her across the playing field.

'Why are you sitting out here all alone under a tree?' Ella snorted. 'Got no friends?'

'I do have friends!' Olivia objected. 'I've got Eliza . . .'

But Eliza had vanished from sight.

'Oooh, an imaginary friend!' Ella mocked.

'She's not imaginary . . .' Olivia began, but she realised it was impossible to explain. Ella would never believe her. And, in a way, she was relieved her sister couldn't see the red-haired girl. Ella had enough friends without taking Eliza too.

At that moment the bell rang and they headed back into school. Olivia sat by herself for the rest of the day and she walked home alone too, while Ella strolled and giggled all the way to their front door with her new group of friends.

'I'm in the kitchen, girls!' Mrs Campbell called to her daughters as they came in. 'I've made after-school treats!'

As they ate their chocolate cake, Mrs Campbell told Olivia what she'd found out about Pemberley Stables.

'It turns out they've been abandoned for as long as anyone can remember. Over the years there have been a few people who've tried to start a riding school and make a go of it there, but for some reason they've always left again.'

Olivia thought she might know why everyone had been scared off. Hadn't Eliza mentioned something about Horace spooking people to cause trouble?

'So, if nobody owns the stables, is it okay if I go and hang out there?' Olivia asked.

Mrs Campbell frowned. 'What on earth would you do that for?'

'I like it there,' Olivia said. 'It's fun looking around the old stables and thinking about all the horses who used to live there.'

'Well, I suppose it's only just down the lane,' Mrs Campbell said, 'but I want you home by dinnertime.'

As she walked to the stables, Olivia thought about her mother's words. Sure, the others had failed, but if Olivia and Eliza could break the spell, then they could restore the stables and bring all the horses back to life and even start their own riding school!

They would do it together just like it said in the spell. One horse at a time.

It was time to convince Bad Bess to give up her life of crime.

Chapter Six

Olivia turned up at the stables with surprises for Eliza and Bess.

'New clothes!' Eliza was delighted as she put on the T-shirt and jeans. 'Look at me!'

'*And chocolate cake! How scrummy!*' the black mare proclaimed when they stepped through her stall doors. '*Thank you, Livvy! I was starving. I get quite hungry from galloping.*

Being a highway horse is very demanding.'

'Aaah,' Olivia said, 'yes, that's what I came here to speak to you about actually, Bess. Because, the thing is, as I said before, I really think you should give up stealing. It's very naughty. You know, if you got caught, you could be arrested and even sent to prison.'

'Ha ha ha!' Bess kicked her legs up and rolled about on the straw with laughter. *'They'd never catch me. I'm the fastest horse on the highway!'*

'It's true,' Eliza confirmed ruefully. 'Bess is very swift.'

'Well, what if someone turned you in to the police?' Olivia was desperate now.

'Oooh, telling on me would be dreadfully mean,' Bess said. *'But they could never keep me in prison, could they?'* As she said this, she reared up dramatically on her hind legs and then, with a

single bound, she dashed past Olivia. This time, rather than using the doors of her stall, Bess simply ran straight through the walls. She disappeared like a mist, re-emerging on the other side.

'Ah yes.' Eliza screwed up her face as if she'd forgotten about the mare's ability to disappear at will. 'Good point.'

Out in the corridor they found naughty Bess looking very pleased with her trick.

'*So you see,*' Bess continued, '*there's no need for me to turn over a new leaf.*'

'Indeed there isn't!' a man's voice boomed through the stables.

Olivia turned round. A rather fat and ruddy-cheeked man, dressed in riding breeches, a red coat and long black boots, was striding towards them. He carried his velvet hard hat under his arm and he wore a huntsman's stock round his throat. The stiff white fabric couldn't hide the fact that his neck was wobbling like mad.

'Horace the Hunt Master', Eliza confirmed to Olivia, who had already guessed that this must be him.

'Ignore the girls, Bess!' Horace said. 'This is a big night for you, my dear! A grand caper. The Duchess of Derryshire and her two daughters are travelling the highway this evening. They'll be wearing their best jewels!'

'*Oooooh!*' Bess looked delighted. '*Triple super-booty!*'

'Indeed!' Horace agreed. 'Time to take to the highway once more! We ride at midnight, my dear Bad Bess!'

And, with his head wobbling as if it might topple off at any moment, Horace spun round and swept back out through the stable doors.

Humming to herself, Bess prepared to make magic. With a flick of her tail she was dressed in her mask and velvet cape. Bending down, she gave her teddy bear a kiss. '*Nighty-night, Raymond*,' she said. Then, with another swish of her tail, she turned to leave, only to find Eliza and Olivia blocking the door.

'Bess . . . we need to talk . . .' Olivia began. But the black mare shook her mane defiantly.

'*No!*' she said. '*I'm not listening to you any more! Stealing is fun, even if it is naughty, and I'm the best at it! And that's final!*'

'Bess, you mustn't . . .' Olivia began again. But her words fell on an empty stall because, in a swirl of mist, Bess had bounded clean through the walls. In a thunder of hooves she had gone!

'We need to go after her!' Eliza said. 'They're

going to rob the Duchess of Derryshire when the clock strikes twelve!'

'But it's only five in the afternoon!' Olivia looked outside. The sun had suddenly disappeared and it was pitch-black outside. 'What's just happened?' she asked Eliza.

'Bess is an enchanted horse. When she rides it's always midnight,' Eliza replied.

'In that case I need to get home!'

'You can't go now!' Eliza's face was even paler than usual. 'We have to stop her!'

Olivia groaned. 'We've already tried and Bess wouldn't listen to us one tiny bit. What makes you think we can change her mind when she's out there now on the highway all dressed up like Batman with Horace egging her on?'

'Because,' Eliza whispered in the darkness, 'you know as well as I do that Bess isn't truly naughty.

She's a good pony, deep down at least. It's the spell – and that awful Horace. He's got her in his thrall. He knows that if we can put a stop to Bess's midnight robberies, then she'll be reformed and we'll be one step closer to saving Spellbound Stables. Horace absolutely doesn't want us to succeed!'

'He's in luck then,' Olivia replied, 'because I give up.'

She began heading for the door, but Eliza blocked her path.

'Out of the way, Eliza,' Olivia said. 'You know I can walk straight through you.'

'Please.' Eliza's eyes were filled with tears. 'Livvy, you can't go. I need you. Those horses in the stables need you. Can you imagine how dreadful it is for them to be stuck in time and never truly do the things that real horses do? I know Bess acts very tough, but I've seen her at night tucked up in the straw, whimpering and snuggling Raymond for comfort. She looks so awfully sad, and I know it's because she wants more than anything to be real again. And I can't help her do it on my own, Livvy. The spell is quite clear: *Two brave girls*. That's us, Livvy. You and me.'

Olivia sighed. 'Okay,' she said. 'But where are we going?'

'Oh wonderful!' Eliza said. 'I knew you wouldn't let me down! The Journeyman's Crossroads is the best place! The coachman is bound to drive the carriage that way and Bess will be waiting for him . . .'

Suddenly the room was filled with a thick ghostly fog.

'Eliza? What's going on?'

The fog was so dense that Olivia couldn't even see her own hand in front of her face. When it cleared at last Olivia wasn't in the stable any more.

She was standing in a grove of blackened trees, with moonlight dancing between the branches all around her. Up ahead she could see a long stretch of road leading to a crossroads with an old-fashioned inn. The lights were out in the building. The road was in total darkness. Nobody was about.

'*Hello?*' Olivia's heart was racing. 'Eliza? Where have you gone?'

In the silence an owl hooted a ghostly reply. It was midnight, Olivia was in the middle of nowhere and she was entirely alone.

Chapter Seven

The sound of horseshoes on the road chimed in the cold night air as the horses galloped and the carriage grew nearer. Olivia could hear their snorts as they strained against the harnesses, the creak of the leather and the crack of the coachman's whip lashing high above them in the moonlit sky.

'Eliza!' Olivia shrieked. 'Eliza, help! They're coming!

'Hallo!'

Olivia leaped up in the air in shock! Eliza was right behind her.

'Argh! Stop doing that to me!' Olivia sputtered.

'Oops, sorry!' Eliza said. 'Come on. We need to warn the coachman about the highway horse . . .'

But before they could set off Bad Bess swept into view. She was magnificent as she galloped towards them with her head held high, her glossy black mane flying in the wind.

'Why, it's the girls!' Bess was delighted to see Olivia and Eliza. She stopped immediately and pulled abruptly to a halt beside them. *'Fancy seeing you out here! How lovely! Have you come to watch me rob the rich?'*

'No, Bess! We've come to stop you!' Olivia said.

Bess whinnied a laugh. *'Stop me? Oofy-goofy! Don't be a silly-billy! This is what I do! I'm a highway horse! Anyway, the carriage is coming and I'd best be off! Toodle-ooooooo!'*

With a dramatic flick of her black cape, Bess leaped forward. She galloped to the middle of the road until she was right smack in the path of the carriage. Then she reared up on her hind legs in a magnificent fashion and called out in a voice that boomed through the night air, *'Stand and deliverrrrrrr!!!'*

'Goodness!' Eliza exclaimed with admiration. 'She is good, isn't she? She's totally fearsome!'

'Never mind how good she is!' Olivia said crossly. 'Come on, Eliza! We have to stop her!'

The two girls began to run towards Bad Bess and the carriage but, before they could even reach the crossroads, there came the sound of a hunting horn.

Tan-tah-rah! Tan-tah-rah! came the trumpet's blare. And then there were other noises too: the baying of hounds and the thunder of hooves, and suddenly, in front of Olivia's eyes, a hunt materialised.

Olivia had never seen a fox hunt of any kind, ghostly or real, before. They were outlawed these days, after all, and she could immediately see why.

The first creature that pelted straight at her was the poor, hunted fox. His bright eyes were wild with fright as he ran as fast as he could, his great ginger brush of a tail streaming out behind him.

'*Roo-roo-roo!!*' The hounds came next. A mad, ragtag pack of wagging tails and lolling tongues,

barging and pushing to get past one another, as they followed the scent of the fox. Olivia had to dance and weave as they surged round her.

Then there was a cry of '*Tally-hooooo!*' and Olivia looked up just in time to see Horace the Hunt Master waving his whip as he bore down on her.

He swung the whip like a sword as he rode past on his horse and Olivia only managed to duck in the nick of time.

'Look out!' Eliza called. 'There's more of them!'

Behind Horace, galloping at top speed, came the ghost riders of the hunt. The men in red coats, the ladies riding side-saddle on ghost-grey steeds with black, haunted eyes. The ghost horses champed at their bits and whinnied in fury. Their hooves clattered on the cobbles of the highway as they continued to gallop straight towards Eliza and Olivia!

And then, just as the hunt was almost upon them,

there came the sound of Horace's hunting horn once more. It was a different noise this time, not *Tan-tah-rah!* but three short peeps: *Blart! Blart! Blart!*

And suddenly, in the blink of an eye, all of them – Horace, the horses, the hounds, even the brave little fox – were gone. And Eliza was at Olivia's side, panting, her eyes wide.

'Horace did that on purpose!' Eliza said. 'He wanted to stop us before we got to Bess!'

'We need to hurry!' Olivia said.

The girls ran as hard as they could, but by the time they got to the crossroads they could see they were too late.

Bess had already stopped the coachman and was robbing the coach! Her booty sack was wide open and the Duchess of Derryshire and her two daughters were trembling as they put their prized possessions into it.

'Take pity on us!' the duchess was pleading. 'Take my gold! Take my pearls! But please leave me my darling diamond tiara. It's a family heirloom and I love it so!'

But Bess wasn't having it. *'J'm a mare who doesn't care!'* she bellowed. 'Come on! Take off the tiara and hand it over!'

Bess's eyes were alight. She was ablaze with the excitement of being naughty. And she wasn't done yet.

'Don't talk back. Throw them in the sack!,' she trilled when the duchess's two daughters cried and begged to keep their beloved china dollies.

'This is not going to plan at all,' Eliza said as she watched the mare greedily stashing her ill-gotten gains.

'No,' Olivia agreed grimly. 'It really, truly isn't.'

With her booty sack full to the brim, Bad Bess rose up once more on her hind legs. For a moment her ghostly outline could be seen against the white orb of the moon. And then, with a flash of hooves and a twirl of her black velvet cape, Bess was gone.

Olivia and Eliza were left standing on the foggy road with the baying of the hounds and the haunting laughter of Horace ringing in their ears.

Chapter Eight

Defeated and exhausted, Olivia and Eliza returned to Spellbound Stables, expecting to find Bess there. But the mare wasn't in her stall.

Eliza was puzzled. 'I wonder where she is?'

'Do you hear something?' Olivia said. 'It sounds like rain – but it's coming from inside the tack room.'

Olivia and Eliza swung the tack-room door open to find poor bewitched Bess sitting atop a pile of glittering treasure while Horace skipped about, throwing gold coins into the air, so that the girls fell over both of them in a sparkling shower. 'Isn't a life of crime a grand thing, Bess, my dear? And you're so good at it!'

Bess whinnied with joy. *'I am super-duper, aren't I?'*

Olivia couldn't believe this. 'No, Bess, you're not! Stealing is wrong.'

'Stealing is fun!' Bess giggled.

'That's right!' Horace agreed. 'Never mind the girls, Bess. You're the best and they're just jealous! Here! Try this on . . .'

Horace clasped a diamond necklace round Bess's velvet-black neck.

'Oh fabby!' Bess beamed, admiring herself in a stolen hand mirror. *'Horace, tomorrow night I do so hope we rob someone who has a diamond bracelet to match!'*

'This is impossible,' Olivia groaned as she watched the horse and the Hunt Master glorying in their treasure. She turned to Eliza. 'I did my best, but it's no use. I'm going home.'

'Livvy!'

'Hey?' Olivia looked up from her dinner plate. 'Yes, Mum?'

'I was only asking what's up with you tonight,' Mrs Campbell said. 'You haven't even touched your food. Is something wrong?'

Olivia thought hard about this. 'I have a *friend*,' she said to her mother. 'And this friend has a problem. She's been taking things. Things that don't belong to her.'

'Oh really?' Ella piped up from the other end of the table. 'For starters, we all know you don't have any friends. And, second of all, are you actually making all this fuss about your stupid sweatshirt that I borrowed? Because I only wore it the once and, yes, I got a big splodge of green ink on it and it won't come out, but it's totally not my fault! You are such a stinky telltale, Livvy'

'Ella!' Mrs Campbell was shocked at her eldest daughter's outburst. 'Taking your sister's sweatshirt was wrong! I mean, really! How would you like it, Ella, if someone did that to you? What if somebody came into your bedroom and helped themself to your favourite things?'

Olivia's eyes widened. 'That's it!'

She leaped up from the table. 'Thanks so much, Mum! You're brilliant!'

'Livvy?' Her mother was confused. 'Aren't you going to finish your dinner?'

'I can't,' Olivia said. 'I have to go and help my friend, the one I told you about!'

Ella pulled a face. 'So that whole story wasn't about me taking your sweatshirt? Then why did I confess? Oh rats . . .'

Out on the highway that night Bad Bess was on top form. She reared and she bellowed her catchphrase that made them all quiver: '*Stand and deliver!*'

And deliver they did. By the time her evening's stealing was done, Bess's booty sack was full to the brim.

'Marvellous work, Bess, my dear!' Horace congratulated her. 'Back to your stall for a well-earned rest. I'll see you again tomorrow night.'

'Hooray for me, I'm the most excellent highway horse ever!' Bess hummed merrily to herself as she headed back to the stables.

In her stall she flicked her tail to remove her mask and cape and hung them on their hooks. And then she dressed in her pyjamas and brushed her teeth and settled down in the straw and . . .

Something was very wrong.

'Where is he? Where is he?' Bess bellowed.

Eliza and Olivia stuck their heads round the corner of the loosebox. 'Missing something?' Olivia asked.

'Raymond!' Bess squeaked. *'My teddy! He's gone.'*

She began searching, checking in the straw and

under her rugs, even in her feed bin. The bear was

nowhere to be found.

'*Raymond!*' Bess called out as if the teddy

might hear her cries and come running. '*Raymond!*

Raymond!'

She turned to Eliza and Olivia, her eyes wild with horror. '*You know what's happened, don't you?*'

'What?' Eliza said.

'*He's been . . .*' Bess couldn't bring herself to say it. '*My teddy's been . . . stolen!*'

'Oh!' Eliza said. 'Well, yes, it looks exactly like that's what's happened here.'

'*How could anyone take Raymond?*' Bess muttered as she stomped back and forth. '*Don't they know I need him to fall asleep? Don't they understand how special he is? How much he means to me?*'

'Hmmmm,' Olivia said. 'It must be awful, to have something that you love taken away from you like that. Don't you think, Eliza?' She gave the other girl a wink.

'What? Oh! Oh yes!' Eliza agreed enthusiastically. 'Like, remember, Bess, when you took the duchess's tiara away from her? Or when you took the china dollies from her two daughters?'

Bess stopped stomping. She looked very, very thoughtful indeed. And then she said, *'Do you think that the duchess and her daughters felt as bad when I took their things as I do now that Raymond has been stolen from me?'*

'Well,' Olivia said, 'now that you mention it, Bess, yes. Yes, I do.'

Bess looked horrified. *'But that's awful!'* she cried. *'I would never want anyone to feel as sad as I do right now! How very, very truly terrible!'*

And now she was flitting around the stall once more. She flew back and forth, stamping and fretting, and then she flung herself at the coat hooks where she had hung her cape and mask just a moment before and hastily put them back on again.

'Bess?' Olivia didn't like this one bit. 'Are you going out stealing again?'

'Oh goodness, no!' Bess shook her mane. *'I will never, ever steal again. But that's not enough, don't you see? Oh, I've been such a naughty horse! Livvy and Eliza, you have to help me! We must go now before it's too late!'*

Bess charged out of the stables and back across

the courtyard. The girls followed her to the tack room where Bess had her booty sack out and was stuffing it full of diamonds and gold as fast as she could.

Bess's eyes were shining. She was brimming with excitement.

'*I've found the china dollies too,*' she told the girls. '*But there's so much more to do! Because tonight, when the moon is full, the highway horse is riding. Girls! Quick! Fill the sack! Because I'm taking it all . . .*

'. . . *and I'm giving it back!*'

Chapter Nine

As the girls packed the sack Bess trotted about, getting more and more worked up.

'*There's too much booty!*' she whinnied. '*I can't manage it alone! Livvy and Eliza, you'll have to help me!*'

'Oh yes!' Eliza agreed. 'Grab the sack, Livvy! Let's go!'

'Me? I've never been on a horse before!' Olivia objected, but Bess wasn't listening.

'*Fabby!*' she cooed. '*You'll need masks and capes – I have spares.*'

'But we're not actually robbing anyone,' Olivia pointed out. 'We're doing the opposite.'

'*All the same,*' Bess said, '*it could be difficult to explain that if the police catch us. No, I think it's best if you look the part . . .*'

As Olivia tied on her mask she felt a rush of excitement. 'I can see now how Bess was tempted by a life of crime,' she confessed as she buttoned her velvet cape at her throat.

'*Tally-ho! Tally-ho!*' Bess called to the girls. '*Let's go! Climb on my back and don't forget the sack!*'

As Olivia leaped up on Bess behind Eliza she felt excitement turn her legs to jelly. Her very first go on a horse! She only just had time to wrap her hands in Bess's beautiful mane before the mare went up on her

hind legs dramatically, her front legs pawing at the sky.

'Yikes!' Olivia shrieked. 'I'm sliding off backwards!'

'*Oops, sorry!*' Bess promptly brought all four legs back down. '*All right back there, you two? Goody-goodness! Hey-ho, off we go! Make 'em quiver! Stand and deliverrrrr!*'

She set off at a gallop and Olivia clung on, her velvet cape flapping behind her in the wind. Her heart was racing as they rode through the fog and, when at last it cleared, she saw that they were back at the Journeyman's Crossroads.

'What's the time?' Eliza asked.

'Midnight precisely,' Olivia said.

'*Look!*' Bess swished her tail. '*Here they come!*'

Up ahead, on the highway, the carriage was approaching at breakneck speed.

'Bess?' Eliza said.

'*Yes?*' Bess replied.

'I know you're all ready to go out there and do your thing. And it's just a small point really. But, before we stop the carriage, I wonder what you should say this time? I mean, now that you're not actually robbing people, perhaps *"stand and deliver"* isn't quite the right catchphrase?'

'*Hmmmm*,' Bess mused. 'Good point, Eliza. What do you think, Livvy? What should I say instead?'

'How about "cutey-tooty, I'm returning your booty"?' Olivia offered.

'*Ooooh*,' Bess swished her tail. '*Fabby! That sounds just like me!*'

'Hurry up, Bess!' Eliza urged. 'They're nearly here!'

'*Hang on tight, girls*,' Bess instructed. '*I'm going straight into a gallop. Here we goooooo . . .*'

In the pale starlit evening Bad Bess cast a ghostly

black outline against the silver moon. When they reached the coachman the black mare threw in yet another dramatic rear, but this time Olivia was ready for her and knew to keep her legs on tight and her hands clenched in the mane.

'*Stand and . . .* ' Bess began to shout out her usual line, but Eliza hissed in her ear to remind her.

'Use your new words!'

'*Oh yes, yes.*' Bess was flustered. '*What was it again? Oh, that's right . . . cutey-tooty! I'm returning your booty!* '

'Oh, very good!' Eliza said. 'I like that!'

'*Thanks!* ' Bess swished her tail. '*It's good, yes?* '

'Umm, hello? Are you quite done?' the coachman sighed irritably. 'I mean, I like a bit of a chat as much as the next man, but are you going to rob us or not? Only it would be good if you could get it over with – I've got other customers waiting for this carriage.'

'*Oh sorry,*' Bess apologised. '*I'll be quick, I promise!*'

Bess went straight up to the carriage window and knocked. The window was lowered and inside was none other than the Duchess of Derryshire and her two daughters!

'*Good evening, ladies!*' Bess flicked her magnificent mane. '*I'm back! Did you miss me?*'

The duchess quivered a little. Her two girls, sitting opposite and clutching very sad-looking home-made sock puppets instead of their usual china dollies, took one look at Bess in her mask and cape and promptly burst into tears. 'Not again!' they wailed.

'*No, no, no!*' Bess was horrified. '*I'm not stealing this time! I'm bringing things back! Go on, Livvy! Show them!*'

From the booty sack, Olivia drew out the tiara and the two china dollies and handed them in through the open window.

The duchess's daughters burst into tears even harder at the sight of their beloved dollies and reached out and clutched their treasures with both hands, hugging them tight for all they were worth. At the sight of their stolen possessions being returned, even the duchess began to cry. She gave tiny little hiccupping sobs of joy as she put the tiara back on her head and examined her beautiful diamonds in the rear-view mirror of the carriage.

'Oh, thank you,' she breathed. 'Thank you! This is all so wonderful. I can't tell you how much it means to us. You are the kindest pony I have ever met. Bless you, noble steed!'

Bess's tail was swishing at top speed now, circling behind her like a helicopter. Her eyes were sparkling as brightly as the duchess's very own diamonds.

'This is brilliant, isn't it?' Bess trilled to Eliza and Olivia. *'Whoever knew that doing good could be even more fun than being naughty?'*

And then, with a shake of her magnificent mane, she said, *'There's no time to waste, girls! We have a busy night ahead of us. Hang on tight because . . . Cutey-tooty! We're giving back ALL the booty!'*

That night, the highway rang with the enchanting chime of Bess's flying hooves as she galloped this way and that. She reared up to stop carriage after carriage and bellowed out her spanking new catchphrase as she handed back all of her ill-gotten stash.

'*Here!*' she told a weeping dowager countess. '*Your pearl earrings!*' '*There!*' she told the Bishop of Bottomley. '*Your coin purse and cufflinks!*' '*And for you, Your Highness,*' she told a terrified royal princess, '*this utterly too-fabulous ruby necklace!*'

The princess tried to object. 'Er ... I'm pretty sure this isn't even mine ...'

But Bess wasn't listening. She was already off and running again.

'Everything must go!' she trilled. *'One night only!'*

'Oof. What a night!' an exhausted Bess groaned, as they headed back to the stables at last. *'We did it, girls! Every last precious possession has been returned.'*

'Well, not quite every possession.' Olivia winked at Eliza. 'There's one more special delivery when we get home.'

Sure enough, as a weary Bess trotted through the door of her stall, she found a surprise waiting for her, nestled in the straw.

'Raymond!'

Bess leaped on her teddy and smothered him with kisses.

'*Naughty bear!*' she said sweetly. '*Oh, I
missed you so! Wherever have you been? I was
worried that I'd lost you forever.*'

'Isn't that adorable?' Eliza said as she watched

Bess hugging the teddy. And then she added, 'I wonder where Raymond got to? Do you think he wandered off on purpose?'

Olivia looked at her friend in disbelief. 'You are joking, aren't you, Eliza? It was me! I hid him to teach Bess a lesson.'

But, before Eliza had the chance to reply, something very strange began to happen in Bess's stall. Suddenly Bess began to tremble and soon all the stables were shaking violently, as if an earthquake had struck.

'Bess!' Olivia shrieked. 'What's happening?'

'*Livvy!*' Bess was wide-eyed in horror. '*Oh my! Oh, help me!*'

Olivia raced to her side, but it was too late. Poor Bess gave a final shudder and let go of Raymond as she fell down, down, down . . . sinking like a stone all the way into the straw of the stable floor.

Chapter Ten

Bad Bess had stopped trembling. She lay utterly motionless, her eyes closed.

'Oh, poor pony!' Olivia tried to throw herself down on the straw at the mare's side, but Eliza blocked her way.

'No! Leave her alone!'

'But, Eliza!' Olivia looked at her friend in disbelief. 'We need to help her!'

Eliza shook her head. 'Don't you see, Livvy? We've helped already. Look!'

And then Olivia saw it too. Bess was glowing. The mare was bathed in a magnificent golden aura. The light that shone all around her was so bright it almost seemed to sing. It glowed so powerfully, and with such warmth, that Olivia knew it was good magic. And for a moment, as the light touched all of them, she felt the energy of it, like a million suns ablaze in her heart. And then the light was gone again and Bess had opened her eyes and was planting her front legs in the straw, struggling like a newborn foal to rise to her feet.

Olivia and Eliza were staring at her with their mouths hanging open.

'She's a real pony!' Olivia whispered.

'Well, duh!' Eliza giggled. 'What did you think she was, Livvy' ? A piggy maybe? Or a Jersey cow

perhaps? Of course she's a pony!'

'What I mean,' Olivia clarified, 'is that Bess is a *proper* pony now. She's not enchanted any more. She's, well, she's *alive.*'

Bess gave a snort, as if she didn't believe what she was hearing. And then she shook her mane and swished her tail.

'The spell!' Eliza clapped her hands in glee. 'It's been lifted. We did it! We did it!'

Bess gave her tail another vigorous flick and then pawed at the straw with her front hoof. She began to trot about her loosebox as if to say, *Why, yes! I do appear to be real! How mar-vehh-louse!! A proper pony at last! Look at me! Wa-hey! Spell-free!* But she wasn't speaking, of course. She was a real horse now and thus completely lost for words as most real horses tend to be.

'She's even more beautiful now than she was

before,' Olivia said as she watched the mare shaking out her lustrous mane and swishing her elegant tail. 'Come on, Eliza! Let's take her out into the fields and we can let her really show off her lovely paces!'

Olivia slipped a halter on to Bess, opened the door to the stall and led the mare out into the corridor. Bess stepped out gaily beside her, hooves clattering on the cobbles. But before they could get far the haunted hounds came bounding through the door.

They were everywhere. A pack of panting, unruly beasties, running this way and that with their tongues lolling pink and drooly out of the sides of their mouths, paws scrabbling over the cobbles as they barged past each other, yelping and whimpering with excitement.

'Yikes!' Olivia shrieked. 'Get off me! Bad dogs!'

'These creatures aren't *dogs*.' An icy, disembodied voice brought a chill to the stables. 'They are hunting hounds. You must never, ever refer to my hounds as dogs. Do I make myself clear?'

Amid the rabble of the hounds a plume of spooky mist appeared, and then the mist took solid form and there was a woman standing before Olivia. She was elegantly dressed in hunting clothes, a black velvet riding habit and a velveteen top hat. Her long, silken, russet hair fell in lush waves round her shoulders and Olivia thought that, despite her grim expression, she was very beautiful indeed. Her lips were coloured scarlet in a perfect Cupid's bow, and she had ghostly pale skin and dark sharply arched eyebrows that gave her an imperious look. As the hounds and the fog began to clear she stood in the centre of the stables, as if she owned the place – which, of course, she did.

'Lady Luella?' Olivia asked.

'Aaah, you know who I am.' Lady Luella arched a brow. 'Clever child! Then you should also know that these are my stables.'

'Oh, I know all about you,' Olivia replied. 'And I think it's just awful what you did! Who would put a spell on poor, innocent ponies?'

'Really! The insolence! Speaking to me like that!' Lady Luella glared at Olivia. 'Be careful, little girl. You're not one of us. You are a human child.'

Olivia felt the threat behind Luella's words, but she gulped down her fear and then she said, 'The magic isn't as powerful as you think, Lady Luella. Bess is free now. And soon all the ponies will be because we're going to save them.'

Lady Luella's face darkened. '"*We're* going to save them"?' she said. 'Who is this *WE* that you speak of?'

'Eliza and me!' Olivia said. 'We're the two brave girls, just like it says in the spell on the wall.'

As soon as she said these words, Olivia realised she hadn't seen Eliza in ages. In fact, not since Lady Luella arrived. Her friend must have remained behind, hidden in Bess's stall.

'Eliza?' Lady Luella looked quite beside herself. 'Why didn't you say that Eliza was here with you? Where is she? Oh, where is she? Eliza? Eliza!!'

'I'm here, Mama.'

Eliza emerged from Bess's stall and came reluctantly out into the corridor to join them. Olivia thought her friend looked very shaken, anxious and even paler than usual. It was almost as if she'd seen a ghost, which, in a way she had.

Lady Luella's eyes welled with tears at the sight of her daughter. 'Eliza,' she said softly. 'Goodness . . .

whatever are you wearing?'

'Oh, the clothes? Livvy gave them to me. I quite like them actually.'

'Why don't you stop this nonsense and come home to the manor with me?' Lady Luella said.

'Because,' Eliza said firmly, 'I will never leave, not while a single pony remains spellbound! Please, Mama, I beg of you, lift the spell!'

'You know I would if I could!' Lady Luella's eyes were filled with tears. 'but the Pemberley Witch made it impossible.'

Lady Luella reached out to touch her daughter, but her fingers disappeared through Eliza's ghostly figure as if they were both made of smoke.

'If my ponies are stuck here, then I'm staying too!' Eliza was defiant. 'Someone has to take care of them! And, besides, I'm not alone now. I have Livvy. Together we're going to free all the ponies and break the spell once and for all.'

'Ah yes,' Lady Luella said. '*Two brave girls*. Just like it says. But beware: spell-breaking is a dangerous business.'

'Eliza and me, we're going to do it.' Olivia stepped up beside her friend. 'We're going to break the spells until all the ponies and Eliza are alive once more.'

'Is that so?' Lady Luella cocked an eyebrow at Eliza, and Olivia saw the mother and daughter exchange a strange look.

'One spell you've broken,' Lady Luella said. 'The other spells remain. You'll need all your wits about you to break the chain. Farewell, Eliza, dear heart, until we meet again.'

Chapter Eleven

In a swirl of mist, with her hounds baying and scampering all around her, Lady Luella slowly faded away.

'So that's your mum?' Olivia said. 'I don't like to be mean, Eliza, but she's not exactly a bundle of joy, is she?'

She felt sorry for her joke straight away when she realised Eliza was crying. It was very strange to see a ghost weeping. Transparent teardrops slid down Eliza's translucent cheeks, and each one that fell disappeared in a sparkle of light before it could hit the ground.

'She wasn't always this way,' Eliza sniffled. 'In the days before the spell she was my mama, and everything was lovely. But the spell binds her just as much as any of us.'

Eliza turned to Olivia. 'All of it is my fault. If I hadn't gone hunting that day, then these poor ponies would never have been trapped like this.'

'Oh, Eliza!' Olivia had to wipe away her own tears now. 'I would hug you if you weren't a ghost! You are the bravest, sweetest, kindest girl that I know and it is utterly NOT YOUR FAULT. You've been blaming yourself for too long now, and you must stop. Together we're going to break the spell. *Two brave girls* – that's us, remember? You and me, we'll turn the tables. One by one, we're going to save every single horse in these stables. We're going to bring your horses back!'

'Oh, Livvy!' Eliza's eyes were shining. 'Do you really think so?'

There was a rather loud and tetchy whinny at that point that snapped both girls briskly back to reality. Bess was prancing about the corridor, tossing her mane and swishing her tail as if to say, *Harrumph! This is all very touching, but in case you both hadn't noticed there is now a real-live horse that needs taking care of!*

'I suppose it's understandable that she's keen to go in the fields,' Olivia said, laughing, as they led Bess outside. 'She's been cooped up now for some two hundred years or so!'

Bess was virtually dancing on the spot as she waited for Olivia to open the gate and let her loose. And the minute she was free she gave a wild buck and then reared up to turn a pirouette on her hind legs.

'I'm glad she didn't do that when we were riding her!' Olivia said.

'Ooh, she's having so much fun!' Eliza was clapping in delight as Bess broke into a canter and then a gallop, tearing about the field like crazy.

And then, all of a sudden, just like that, Bess's wild galloping was over.

'What's wrong?' Olivia asked. 'Why has she stopped?'

Eliza giggled. 'Because she's hungry!'

It was true. Bess had finally noticed that there was all this yummy grass to eat right under her very hooves. And so she promptly gave up on her high-spirited antics and threw her head down and began to munch. While she grazed contentedly the girls went back inside the stables and Eliza showed Olivia how to muck out Bess's stall and how to cover the floor with fresh straw and put clean water in her trough and mix her a hearty feed of oats and chaff.

'It's going to be a lot of work running these stables once we bring all the horses back,' Olivia grunted, as she pushed the wheelbarrow full of muck out to the dung heap outside.

'That's true,' Eliza said, sitting on the top of some hay bales with her legs dangling. 'And I'm sorry I can't do anything useful. You know, being ghostly and all means I can't lift a finger!'

'How convenient!' Olivia said. And then she instantly regretted the joke when she saw how sad Eliza looked.

'I know you'd love to be able to help me,' she said to her friend. She looked around the stables. 'Maybe one day, when they're all back in their looseboxes and the spell is finally broken?'

Olivia put the wheelbarrow away. 'There!' she said. 'Bess's stall is all done. One horse down . . .'

'. . . and the rest to go!' Eliza leaped down off the hay bales. 'What do you say, Livvy? Are we ready for the next one?'

'Definitely!

NEXT IN THE SERIES . . .

Spellbound Ponies

Sugar and Spice

It was such a lovely day for a picnic! Olivia had a spring in her step as she walked from her house to Pemberley Stables with her lunchbox packed to the brim with ham sandwiches and chocolate cake.

The stables, ancient and ivy-clad, looked for all the world as if nobody had set foot inside them for centuries. But Olivia had been here before and she knew that the heavy wooden doors would slide open easily for her. She stepped inside and admired her handiwork. She'd been on a cleaning spree lately. The musty cobwebs were gone and the cobblestones in the corridor had been polished until they gleamed.

'Eliza? It's me!' Olivia whispered into the gloom. 'I've brought us picnic treats. Sandwiches and cake!'

'Cake? Oh, how glorious!' The voice came from right behind her and Olivia spun round. Standing there, where a moment ago there had been nothing but thin air, was a girl dressed in an old-fashioned white Georgian nightgown with a tangled mass of red curls tied up in a bun and bright green eyes. She looked about the same age

as Olivia, which was nine, but, in fact, she was two hundred and nine on account of the fact that she was a ghost!

'Oh, not those old clothes again, Eliza!' Olivia squeaked. 'I've bought you a new set to wear,' she said, handing over a bundle of new things. 'And don't sneak up on me like that!'

'Oops, sorry, Livvy!' The red-haired girl giggled. 'I didn't mean to startle you. And it's frightfully nice of you to bring me clothes, and lunch . . .'

At that moment there was a whinny from inside the first stall and a beautiful jet-black pony stuck her head out over the bottom door. 'Bess, on the other hand,'

Eliza grinned, 'simply cannot wait to munch on some scrummy pony food!'

'Well, she's in luck!' Olivia said. 'The hay is on its way. I ordered a bale from **Harrow's Horse Feed** this morning.'

As she said this, there was a honk outside.

'Hay, hay, hooray!' Olivia said. 'That'll be the delivery now!'

She bounded outside and found Mr Harrow standing in the driveway, a clipboard in his hand, looking quite confused.

'Are you the girl who ordered the hay?' he asked.

'Yes!' Olivia said brightly. 'Can you stack it inside, please? I've cleared a space.'

Mr Harrow still looked puzzled as he grabbed a bale from the truck.

'I didn't think they were any horses in these stables,' he said as he lugged it inside. 'They've been abandoned for as long as anyone can remember.'

'Well, not any more!' Olivia said cheerily. 'We've only got Bess right now, but we're expecting lots more ponies very soon.'

'Is that so?' said Mr Harrow. 'Well, you'll be needing more hay then!'

'More?' Olivia had already emptied the entire contents of her piggy bank to buy this one bale.

'Oh yes,' Mr Harrow said seriously. 'Ponies will eat you out of house and home, you know!'

Mr Harrow threw the bale down and headed back out. He was about to leave when he spotted the words carved into the stone wall half hidden beneath the overgrown ivy. 'Hang on a minute –' he pushed the leaves aside – 'there's something written under here . . .'

Mr Harrow read the words out loud.

The deepest magic binds these stables
Unless two brave girls can turn the tables.
The curse on each horse must be found,
Then break their spell to be unbound.

'What's that all about then? Is it a poem?'

'Erm, yes, something like that,' Olivia replied.

In fact, it wasn't a poem at all. It was a spell. And

Olivia knew the spooky story behind it only too well.

It had all begun two hundred years earlier when Lady Luella, owner of Pemberley Manor, had decided to go fox-hunting. Her daughter, Eliza, had begged to come with her on the hunt. Eliza was an excellent rider and everything was going brilliantly until they struck a rabbit hole at a hedge jump and Eliza's pony, Chessie, lost his footing and fell.

Eliza's death so devastated Lady Luella that she had decided to punish all the ponies in the stables. She had paid the Pemberley Witch to cast a curse over them all and ever since then the stables had been spellbound. The witch's magic kept the poor ponies trapped forever in time!

Except there was a weakness in the witch's spell. *Two brave girls* could break the curse, and Olivia, who was very brave indeed, was one of those girls. The other was Lady Luella's daughter, Eliza. After her terrible accident, Eliza had refused to leave the Spellbound ponies, staying on at the stables as their groom, and that was how she met Olivia.

When Olivia had helped Eliza to free Bad Bess, the naughty highway pony, from the witch's spell, the two girls had become firm friends.

Having a ghost as a friend was a lot of fun, but there were drawbacks. For starters there was Eliza's rather worrying habit of coming and going in a magical *poof*! Right now, as Mr Harrow stood in the doorway of the darkened stables, Olivia became aware that a spooky swirl of mist was starting to rise – a sure sign that Eliza was about to mystically materialise! Yikes! Olivia was pretty sure she was the only one who could actually see this happening, but she wasn't taking any chances!

'It's been lovely chatting with you about poetry and all that,' Olivia said, hurrying Mr Harrow out

to his truck and helping him by opening the door,
'but I've got a pony to feed!' . . .

To be continued . . .

CAN THEY SAVE THEM ALL?

Spellbound PONIES
Wishes and Weddings

STACY GREGG

Out Now

CAN THEY SAVE THEM ALL?

Spellbound PONIES
Sugar and Spice

STACY GREGG

Out Now

CAN THEY SAVE THEM ALL?

Spellbound PONIES
Magic and Mischief

STACY GREGG

Collec

them all!